Silly Sally

by Audrey Wood

Harcourt, Inc.

ORLANDO   AUSTIN   NEW YORK   SAN DIEGO   TORONTO   LONDON

For information about permission to reproduce
selections from this book, please write Permissions,
Houghton Mifflin Harcourt Publishing Company 215
Park Avenue South NY NY 10003.

Wood, Audrey.
Silly Sally/by Audrey Wood.
p.   cm.
Summary: A rhyming story of Silly Sally, who makes many
friends as she travels to town—backwards and upside down.
ISBN 0-15-274428-2
[1. Humorous Stories.   2. Stories in rhyme.]   I. Title.
PZ8.3.W848Si   1992
[E]—dc20   91-15939

SCP 34 33
4500473685

The paintings in this book were done in Winsor & Newton
watercolors on Arches watercolor paper.
The display type was hand lettered by the illustrator,
based on a rendering by Brenda Walton, Sacramento,
California.
The text type was set in Adroit Light by
Thompson Type, San Diego, California.
Color separations by Bright Arts, Ltd., Singapore
Printed and bound by South China Printing, China
Production supervision by Warren Wallerstein and
Ginger Boyer
Designed by Michael Farmer

Printed in China

For Ann and Warren Wallerstein

Silly Sally went to town,
walking backwards, upside down.

On the way she met a pig,
a silly pig,

they danced a jig.

Silly Sally went to town,
dancing backwards, upside down.

On the way she met a dog,
a silly dog,

they played leapfrog.

Silly Sally went to town,
leaping backwards, upside down.

On the way she met a loon,
a silly loon,

they sang a tune.

Silly Sally went to town,
singing backwards, upside down.

On the way she met a sheep,
a silly sheep,

they fell asleep.

Now how did Sally get to town,
sleeping backwards, upside down?

Along came Neddy Buttercup,
walking forwards, right side up.

He tickled the pig
who danced a jig.

He tickled the dog
who played leapfrog.

He tickled the loon
who sang a tune.

He tickled the sheep
who fell asleep.

He tickled Sally,
who woke right up.

She tickled Neddy Buttercup.

And that's how Sally got to town,

walking backwards, upside down.